How the Elephant got his Trunk

A Shangaan and Venda Tale

Retold by Andrea Florens

Illustrated by Angela Sinclair

Long, long ago in Africa, the elephants that roamed the veld looked much like they do today. They were the biggest of all the animals with huge bellies and heavy legs. The elephants had enormous ears, and two white tusks. But there was something quite different about the elephants all those many years ago...

They did **not** have a long **trunk**!
Instead all the elephants had short,
and rather *funny*, little noses.

Feeding was a **difficult** task for such **cumbersome** creatures. They would have to **bend down** on their knees and **eat** the grass. Drinking was also not very easy. The elephants would have to wade into the water and **kneel** down to quench their thirst.

munch
munch

One day, the herd of elephants had wandered far in search of water.

Eventually they found a **new river** and before long, they were kneeling in the cool water to gulp down as much as they could.

What the elephants **did not** know was that
the river was home to an **old crocodile**. The crocodile was
big and **strong**, and always **hungry**.

When the crocodile saw these enormous creatures,
he was very happy. "One of these big animals would make
a lovely meal!" he thought as he swam slowly closer,
with only his eyes peering out from under the water.

The elephants did not notice the greedy crocodile approaching – too busy were they slurping up the water on their bent knees. As Crocodile got closer he slowly opened his long jaws... wider, and wider until... SNAP!

He **clamped** his mouth over a young elephant's nose!

The **poor** young elephant got **such a fright** that he immediately pulled backwards to free himself. The crocodile himself was **also** surprised...

usually catching a creature was easy work.

And so the struggle began. Back and forth they tugged.
Sometimes it looked as though the crocodile might win, but then
the elephant tugged with all his might, and he managed to pull

the crocodile onto the riverbank. But then the crocodile would pull
the other way again. The other elephants looked on anxiously,
all cheering loudly when the elephant seemed to be winning.

Soon a **crowd** of other animals gathered at the water.
Monkeys, zebras, buck, warthog, flamingos and many more –
all cheering the elephant on because at one time or another
they had all lost a friend to the jaws of the
nasty crocodile.

The sun was setting, and after **struggling** for **many hours**, the **exhausted** elephant made a final BIG tug, and

WHUMP – landing on his bottom – he was free! The angry crocodile disappeared back into the depths of the water.

The animals on the riverbank
cheered and rejoiced,
so happy that the
young elephant was safe
and that someone had
finally beaten the ugly old croc.

Eventually when all the other animals had left,
the tired young elephant noticed that the older elephants
were whispering to each other worriedly.

His younger friends on the other hand were sniggering and laughing. His sore and throbbing nose was what they were all talking about.

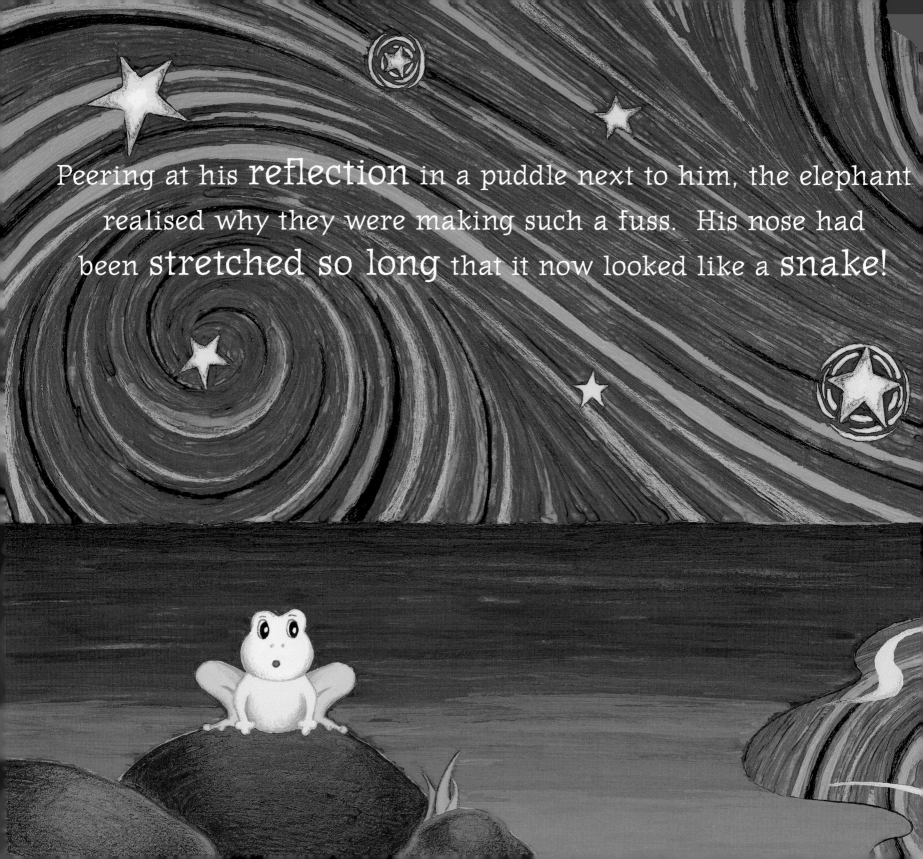

Peering at his reflection in a puddle next to him, the elephant realised why they were making such a fuss. His nose had been stretched so long that it now looked like a snake!

While the young elephant was rather upset with this strange new nose, he did realise however, that he was lucky to be alive. And so he decided there and then to make the best of his long and winding snout.

And that's exactly what he did. Soon it was the other elephants that were feeling sorry for themselves. With elephant's new trunk, he was able to reach the highest branches for juicy leaves. And no longer did he kneel to drink, he could simply slurp up the water with his fantastic new nose!

It **wasn't long** before the other elephants made their way back to that riverbank to have a **tug-of-war** with the old crocodile.

One by one they came back with their stretched noses. And **each elephant** discovered how wonderful it was to have a **long trunk** instead of a short and stumpy nose.

From that time onward all elephants were born with
a **long, winding** and **very useful** trunk.

Crocodiles **still** try to catch elephants every now and then. But **luckily** it's usually the elephants that win!

Produced by Art Publishers (Pty) Ltd
Durban, Johannesburg, Cape Town